365
MAN LAWS
TO LIVE BY

BRETTE CLARK

MITCHELLANDMORGAN
PUBLISHING HOUSE

Contents

Forward

The Laws

About the Author

Forward

"It started as a hashtag between friends on Twitter that turned into a whirlwind of witty and slightly offensive Man Laws between friends. Now I've decided to share them with all the men of the world. Take heed if you want to keep your man status in full effect."

-Brett Clark

1. A man shall never use the shorthand "Cum" as a quicker way to say the word "Come" or "Cometh" when texting another man.

2. As a man, tis okay to eat Wheat Thins, but not so much as to actually purchase them.

3. No man is allowed to watch women's television networks unless there is an immovable ball and chain shackled to thine foot.

4. No man shall work for an employer whose flagship products are lotions, scented oils, perfume, candles, nail polish, makeup, or body scrubs. It is never cool saying the word "honeysuckle".

5. The root word of emoji is emotion. Men don't use them. Men don't have them.

6. Bringing sand to a beach is permissible only if it leads to a first or second time "score" after leaving the event, or "beach".

7. Unless a man is training for the Olympics, under no circumstance, should thine own a pair of bikini

briefs. As a matter of fact, thou hasn't the slightest clue what a pair even looks like.

8.   "Sex In The City™" is the act of having intercourse in a metropolitan area. Not a television show, play, book or movie.

9.   Unless you will be appearing on a nationally televised dance program with celebrity judges, you have never done, or intend to do "the splits".

10.   TyPiNg LiK3 ThIS is unacceptable in any and all forms of communication. Any physical harm that results is one's own fault.

11.   If a man raises thine open hand to slap another man in the face, thine slap recipient's immediate reaction should be a three-piece combo to the perpetrator's jaw bone, rib cage and nasal cavity.

12.   If thou doesn't know who's playing, do not ask. Asking will result in banishment from the room and immediate kitchen

duty. However, asking the score is acceptable.

13. When using a public urinal, one must keep one's eyes on the road. Any eye contact can briefly take place at the sink after business is handled. And by briefly, we're talking (.05) secs.

14. The acronym "OMG" stands for "one more game". It can be uttered when suffering from shortness of breath after a crushing sports loss.

15. Thou shall not hear interesting news of your colleagues and decide it's your duty to share with other colleagues. Men were born with the inability to gossip. Shall you ever feel the urge, check thine self before you wreck thine self.

16. Note to women: It is a blatant Man Law violation to place thine hands on your man's bottom during public or private displays of affection. Any breach of this law shall result in a mandatory threesome to gain his man privileges back.

17. The only instance where two able bodied males are allowed to transport on a two wheeled vehicle together (i.e. a motorcycle), is with the use of a sidecar, Batman and Robin style.

18. If thou owns a pair of rollerblades, reach into thine pocket, grab a dollar, use said dollar to hold thine place in this book, stop reading immediately, go grab thine rollerblades, start up thine car, then go toss them in the nearest lake to be found. A dumpster just won't do. You need no evidence.

19. Kissing is quite okay and can lead to other fun activity, but puckering thine lips in any photographed work is completely and utterly unacceptable.

20. If a member of the secret society of Man Law's ever catches a male specimen with the slightest shade of makeup on thine face or body, said male should hope the day is October 31st or "Football Sunday".

21. Okay yeah, you've tried hula hooping... when you were eight yrs old... and you sucked at it. Thou shall be granted with a pass.

22. It's not really common practice to "notice" a smudge of food on another man's face. But it's totally forbidden to even think about wiping it off.

23. There is way less discomfort in sleeping on a floor, as opposed to the discomfort of sharing a bed with another man. The option of sleeping feet to head shouldn't be an option, unless this is a father to son or brother to brother situation (still debatable).

24. Never shall a man sit to pee. If one sits in belief that one will defecate and only urinates, one must remain sitting until one boo boos.

25. When standing, a man's weight shall remain centered at all times. Never shall a man shift his weight onto either of his hips.

26. No violation here, but it's just really not manlike to ever request

a "doggy bag". If on a date and can't finish all of your man food, remember you can always announce that you're going give thine leftovers to a homeless person in need.

27. A man shall never buy, watch, subscribe or borrow a DVD which is intended to give the viewer better abdominals.

28. A loose handshake is equivalent to giggling; it's just not manly.

29. The text shorthand "lol" shall only be used to soften the blow of an otherwise offensive or male chauvinistic comment. Never in the history of digital messaging, has it ever been okay for a man to use "lol" stand-alone.

30. Men don't consume small meals. A man shall eat until fully satisfied and self professed as full.

31. A man shall not shave below the neck. Some trimming is acceptable, but never shaving.

32. Men don't plant or maintain gardens. If a man is in the mood to

grow vegetables, said man shall go full out, buy a few acres of land, and become a farmer.

33. Men don't knit. Knitting is really ludicrous.

34. Unless thou is stranded on an island with nothing but sand, palm trees and an ice cream truck, popsicles are a complete and utter no-go.

35. Men don't compliment men on anything except sports accolades, overpriced gym shoes and the women they've conquered. This list includes, but not limited to: physique, facial features, tattoos, hair, attire, singing voice, personality, etc.

36. It is okay to share thine sexual exploits with comrades, only until 1) thou is diagnosed with feelings of love 2) thou hath dated a dame for longer than 120 days 3) thou realizes that said dame is actually a monstrosity picked up in a drunken stupor.

37. Mankind will never understand the science behind this one, but during moments of extreme jubilation in professional sporting events, an athlete may from time to time take it upon himself to swat another athlete on the backside. This is only allowed due to the sheer volume of backside swats over decades of professional sports. In conclusion, unless thou is a professional athlete, thine hands and other various extremities shall remain at least three feet from all other male backsides at all times.

38. A man shall never clap or applaud vertically and/or symmetrically. Even in the comfort of thine own home, this is cannot and will not happen.

39. No man is allowed to buy bottled water at any amateur or professional sporting event. If said man happens to be at thine son's little league game and no beer is available for purchase, said man must drink from the same cooler as his son's team. It is

acceptable and encouraged to pretend to give said son coaching advice upon the initial attempt at quenching thirst.

40. Upon stepping on another man's foot in a crowded environment, if man is still within arm's length simply place thine flattened palm on the victim's back for no longer than two seconds and utter a simple "my bad". If the stepee is out of arm's length, then said violator must quickly tap thine own chest twice, accompanied by a quick head nod that insinuates "my bad."

41. Never ever communicate your frustrations with another man via text message when both parties are within 200 feet.

42. Patience is not a virtue. Very little good fortune comes to men who wait.

43. When approaching a high trafficked exit on an interstate, and a line forms, no man shall find themselves more than seven cars from the exit. Said driver must

display aggressive driving measures until an appropriate placement in line is achieved. If a woman is driving and a man is riding shotgun, said man must encourage driver to wait at the back of the line, put the car in park, and trade places with man. The aforementioned Man Law shall then take its course. If a man is riding in the back seat and no man is present in the front of the vehicle, his man status must be revoked until further review.

44. Never sip beer. If a man is not sure whether he is a sipper or not, just simply reach out and grab thine beer bottle. Is said beer bottle still cold? If thine answer is "yes", thou are still declared a man. If thine wretched answer is "no", thou hath been sipping beer and are quickly approaching banishment.

45. The only hair missing from thine eyebrows shall be from natural follicle displacement. If any man shall ever think about getting thine brows shaved, said man

must accompany such arching of
the brows with lip gloss and
eyeshadow, and seriously
consider getting a sex change.

46.   Men never clean as they go. All
      pizza boxes, beer cans, video
      game casings, peanut shavings,
      and any other man trash shall
      remain stacked and/or scattered
      everywhere until the entire male
      bonding session has been
      adjourned.

47.   As a man cometh home from a
      bachelor party, thine script shall
      read as follows, "It was okay. I
      wasn't really enjoying myself
      until we got into a spirited debate
      about whose wife is the hottest.
      Maaan that (bachelor's name) is
      really head over heels about that
      girl."

48.   Men don't cancel activities due to
      inclement weather.

49.   Two men shall never acknowledge
      or reattempt a botched handshake
      greeting. Just accept it and keep it
      moving.

50. No man may ever own a dog smaller than a housecat.

51. If there is a three-seater sofa in the room, and three men desire to sit down, all three must briefly and telepathically play a round of musical chairs as if there were only two chairs remaining.

52. While intoxicated, it's cool to debate about who has the bigger Johnson, but never cool to try and prove it.

53. Thou shall never pull roadside to help another able-bodied man to change thine tire.

54. Men don't go on diets. They either eat healthy or they don't.

55. If a female specimen gives a man a jar to open and said man is unable to open said jar, the said man's Man Status may be revoked for 11 to 30 days.

56. Individual pictures of other men in thine phone are only reserved for thine son or father.

57. There are lots of issues that a man shall be concerned with throughout thine day. Correcting thine posture shall not be one of them.

58. No man shall use a blanket to keep warm during the daytime, unless said man has a night job and must get his shuteye during daylight hours.

59. Some men are breast men. Other men are butt men. Some are both. None are neither.

60. No two men are allowed to enter a revolving door together.

61. When entering a revolving door, one must only push with one hand and avoid shuffling feet to accommodate the small spacing.

62. It is okay to occasionally eat ice cream, accompanied by another dessert, such as apple pie or a brownie, but thou shall never express to another human that thine hath a favorite ice cream flavor.

63. Sit-down restaurants with one or more buddies is not forbidden, but highly discouraged outside of lunch hours and televised sporting events.

64. While in a vehicle with other men, the only acceptable genres of audio entertainment are Heavy Metal Rock, Trap Music, Tupac, or the Rocky theme song.

65. Things men don't share with one another: blankets, umbrellas, clothes, meals, gossip and wives. One male party will just have to be wet, naked, hungry, uninformed and/or free from the tyranny of a wife.

66. Open armed man hugs will be reserved for immediate family members only, in addition to weddings and funerals (with 3 sec rule). Nowhere else. In the instance where a full-frontal hug is deemed appropriate, belt buckles should not ever touch.

67. If you must buy your pal a birthday gift, it must be an item

that will possess zero sentimental value for a minimum of 10 years.

68.   Ed Sheeran. The guy knows what he's talking about. You can be a fan. Don't play yourself.

69.   Thou shall not get wasted from drinking wine.

70.   Although not outlawed, it's not common practice to walk around another man barefoot. It would be common practice to immediately put some shoes on.

71.   There is only one letter in the alphabet that a man is forbidden to text or type stand-alone. K?

72.   Asking another dude where he bought a particular article of clothing is no different than complimenting him on his smile.

73.   Barring extreme circumstances, such as tragedy or immediately after winning a grueling sports championship, thou shall never cry in front of another man. Not even a sniffle.

74. Thine dog must weigh more than 50 pounds.

75. Under no circumstances shall any man strike a female. However, spankings are fully permitted.

76. Thou shall forever be boggled upon entering "sandals tho" in a search engine and finding that "sandals thong for men" pops right up.

77. There is simply no instance where this collection of consonants and vowels should ever emanate from a man's oral cavity: "cosmo."

78. For men over the age of 19: Dry humping is a fire hazard.

79. If a man finds himself without the assistance of GPS and lost in a particular geographic area, said man must search for an additional 20 minutes using only his manly instincts before sending a female passenger to ask for directions. If there is no female present in the vehicle, then said man must purchase an item and "happen" to

ask for directions while at the register.

80.   If a man accidentally becomes aware that another man's fly is open (preferably through his peripheral vision) this is a violation, but since the damage is already done, he is not allowed to gesture to the subject that his fly is open. That would force said subject to look directly at thine private area and creates a double violation.

81.   Farting is never discouraged, but if one farts in a public area, at least have the decency to look around with an appalled look on your face as if someone around you just let one loose.

82.   Handshakes between males should last no more than 4 seconds. Anything more is considered holding hands and an extreme violation. One thousand one. One thousand two. One thousand three. One thousand four.

83.   Although the members of the secret society of Man Laws haven't a clue why it's prohibited, there's just something very wrong with having your shirt off on your social networking site's avatars.

84.   Writing a handwritten letter to express your feelings will never be deemed manly, although sometimes is a necessary financial move to avoid having to pay a divorce lawyer.

85.   It is fully understood that crying at your own wedding is permitted. With the understanding that you are staring at the last woman you will ever sleep with.

86.   Your preference on boxers or briefs is totally thine own decision, however, the color is not. White, black, grey, or earth tones only. This is a very strict Man Law. All violators will be prosecuted to the full extent of the law.

87.   While driving alone or with a lady friend, it is permitted (not encouraged) to play music

categorized as "love songs". Although you must do so with each window rolled up all the way, and at no more than 55% volume and/or 48 decibels.

88. The only time it's permitted to have your mouth near other man's ear is in a loud environment such as a nightclub, however, one must follow a two inch rule, never use both hands to cuff one's ear, and the topic of conversation must be about how hot the woman are.

89. Sunday is reserved for football, church, and yard work. In that order.

90. There is NO woman law.

91. If you make a store run, you are prohibited from bringing back anything that wasn't already requested by your buddies. i.e. "I was walking through the candy aisle and happened to see your favorite candy bar, so I bought two, one for you and one for me."

92. Never look at a photo of the artist currently known as Prince directly in the eyes.

93. When going to the movies with your buddies, each male must skip a seat when seating themselves. If there is not enough available seating to accommodate this law, said buddies must immediately get their money refunded.

94. Although some men's dancing prowess may impress some women, never will you engage in dance contests between you and your crew.

95. If at the movies with your buddies and are able to abide by Man Law #94, the content of the movie must include one or more of the following: fight scenes, brief or full nudity, guns, car chases, explosions, sports, or a very popular comedian.

96. Although watching the show may be a violation, it is quite acceptable to think that Ellen Degeneres is a hip gal.

97. The only time that it's permissible to take a gal ice skating is if you've known her for four to eight weeks and haven't slept with her yet. This process is called "an act of foreplay."

98. If a man decides to take on a career as a massage therapist, he is never allowed to massage another able-bodied man. It must be understood that when the female therapist at your spa takes the day off from work, so do you, man.

99. Thou shall not wear dress shoes and sweat socks. This is only reserved for Michael Jackson impersonators and males under the age of nine.

100. It has never been allowed for a man to watch adult films with members of the same gender.

101. You bathe standing up. Let us repeat that. It doesn't matter how sore your muscles are, you bathe standing up.

102. Just because Oprah said it, it doesn't make it official.

103. When relieving oneself in a public restroom, no portion of one's buttock shall be visible to the "naked" eye.

104. There shall never cometh a time when a man needeth to arch thine back.

105. While hugs between men may occur during moments of extreme jubilation or sadness, a "behind the back" hug between any two men is extremely forbidden.

106. While locking lips with a particular female specimen, regardless of how hot she is, and regardless of the amount of pleasure induced, it is never acceptable to "moan".

107. The only instance where a man is allowed in a nail shop is upon the occasion in which a female counterpart he has dated for a period of 5 months or longer, hath no other means of

transportation to her nail appointment. Needless to say, manicures for men hath never and will never be allowed.

108. Upon a physical altercation with another male, after three total pushes have been exchanged between the two, the next exchange must be a strike to the face of the opposition. Another shove will place both subjects in the penalty box for simulating powder puff football.

109. It is only permissible for a man to order a fruit flavored alcoholic beverage, if said subject is wearing swim trunks or an all white linen outfit and is located within a two mile radius of a beach resort.

110. In the court of Man Law, the statement "I was Drunk" will have the same effect as   an insanity plea (reduced punishment) in standard court provided the defendant's   blood alcohol level exceeds .10.

111.   A crying woman driver is more
        of a driving hazard then a blind
        man driving under the influence.
        When thou hath spotted such a
        detriment to society, please call
        the authorities and avoid at all
        costs.

112.   To a man, there is absolutely
        nothing in a Soap Opera of
        entertainment value.

113.   Often times, two men will settle
        their differences by deciding it's
        best to knock each other's head
        off. This is common practice in
        male specimens of almost every
        species on the planet. However,
        it is strict Man Law that one
        shall strike opposing man with
        thine closed fist or elbow.
        Sometimes kneeing and kicking
        is allowed if said opponent is
        getting the best of you. Never is
        it okay to strike a man between
        the area below the waist and
        above the knees. Never.

114.   Checking thine self into a
        hospital for having a cold is like
        crying when a girl dumps you. A

serious case of overreacting. It's just not manlike. You'll be ok... man.

115. The words "I'm sorry" should only emanate from a man's mouth when his main supply of sex is threatened on a temporary to permanent basis. By temporary, we mean, more than 72 hours.

116. Some men are vegetarians. By deciding to severely alter thine diet as such, said plant nibbling male is in agreement with the rest of the male population that meat-eating men are more dominant and "most likely to succeed".

117. No matter where you are, never stretch your leg in any awkward position in an attempt to adjust thine self. If thou are not sure what thou will look like in the adjustment attempt, just go for the gusto and manually adjust thine crotch. It looks more natural.

118.   If two or more males arrive at a party by a single car, and the driving male is hooking up with a girl, it is the responsibility of the other male(s) to find other ways home. (The exception to this law is if the driver is hooking up with his own girlfriend, the law is then void and the driver still holds full responsibility of driving his friends home).

119.   Some things a man accomplishes should not be rewarded or applauded, as they are normal obligatory tasks that are expected to happen. Bragging about getting an exotic dancer's phone number is like bragging about graduating high school.

120.   Thine BBQ grill is a sacred place. Thou are deemed the only one in thine household who is allowed place hands on it. Occasionally, your buddies my glide their hands across it in admiration, but they are never allowed to actually fire it up. We highly recommend you rig it so that it

will only function through a
hand print sensor and voice
activation.

121. Men don't take bathroom breaks
together. Every man present in
a public restroom while you are
handling thine business, shall be
a stranger to you. Upon the
instance that you run into a
familiar fellow inside the
restroom, an appropriate head
nod shall suffice until both
subjects are outside of the
restroom and are able to engage
in awkward small talk
afterwards.

122. Group pictures among men shall
be reserved for family reunions,
team sporting events,
fishing/hunting expeditions
(with the hunted specimen) and
prison.

123. There are certain professions in
which it is of benefit to be seen
mingling with certain
celebrities. It is not man-like to
ask another male categorized as
a celebrity to take a picture with

you, although full-time event promoters, PR professionals, up-and-coming recording artists, politicians and actors all have a pass on this one.

124. If you gather intelligence that a close buddy of yours is dating a known harlot, you are allowed to issue one warning of stupidity. Nothing more. Most men learn life lessons by not listening to friends and falling directly on their face.

125. If a video game controller is sitting on top of a book, that is on top of a pillow, that is on top of a laptop computer, that is sitting on a man's lap; another man grabbing said controller would be an extreme violation of grabbing/touching an object located on another man's lap.

126. Vision is key. Image is everything. But color contact lenses will have you banned.

127. When at social events that allow for casual attire, thou shall not

smile in any photographs taken with other male specimen.

128. It is customary and encouraged for all men to do at least 100 sit-ups and push-ups before any 1st, 2nd, 3rd, 4th, 5th, 6th, or 7th date. If she hasn't desired to see you naked by then, thou shalt move on and think about increasing push-up regimen to 200 upon dating a new dame.

129. Unbeknownst to most members of the lady gender, men will share stories of sexual conquests with up to three buddies. When asked by a member of the lady gender about this braggadocious trait, a swift and convincing statement of denial must be expressed by said conqueror. Note: This ego boosting custom has been going on since men lived in caves.

130. Whomever man published the first use of the word "platonic", is one of the greatest fiction writers of all time.

131.   Thou shall not ever flinch while watching any horror film. Especially in the presence of an attractive member of the lady gender.

132.   Men are only allowed to take a particular human act "personal" for up to 8 secs before remembering that thine is a man and not allowed to take things personal.

133.   There are approximately 45 ways to appropriately close a phone conversation without having to say "bye bye".

134.   During moments of passion with a woman between the ages of 18 and 23, always attempt to remove her brazier with one hand. If executed successfully this could really impress her and enhance the moment. If you can't execute in less than 10 seconds, use two hands. If another 10 seconds goes by and it's still on, just rip said bra off. Never ask for help.

135.   Sometimes in order to fully enjoy oneself while watching television programs, a man must rest thine hand(s) inside his pants. Studies have shown, this is a customary practice all over the world.

136.   It's just not cool to let her pump her own gas... unless you have evidence that she's been going through your phone spying on you.

137.   There shall not be many occurrences in a man's lifetime, where he finds himself watching a movie at home with another member of the male species.

138.   If you have kids, and happen to take them out for breakfast, never verbally order the Rooty Tooty Fresh & Fruity for them. Just simply point at it.

139.   In the event that five or more buddies are headed out, take two vehicles. Visualize yourself and two other grown men in the same back seat. Touche´. This is mandatory.

140. Never shall a man tell another man "Good Night".

141. No man shall try to avoid coat check by tying thine coat around thine waist in a nightclub.

142. Unless posing after draining a free throw, a man's wrist is never allowed to break more than a 20 degree angle.

143. In some night clubs, male club goers may engage in a phenomenon called "making it rain" where they toss money in the air for female specimen to catch and keep. It is extremely important that you not touch any of the showering dead presidents. Such a violation may result in severe case of assault.

144. On severely hot days, it is okay to order a slush at your neighborhood convenient store. However, upon the instance that the slush spills out the hole on the top, just let it naturally fizzle down. Please do not "slurp" the top.

145. The only man allowed to help you tie a tie around thine neck, are thine father and possibly a trained professional at a reputable suit shop. Emphasis on possibly.

146. Prior to 1988, an able bodied man may have had few options other than asking another man to hold his feet while performing sit-ups. Post 1988, this is an extreme Man Law violation.

147. It is rare that a man's priorities for relationships not fall in this order. 1) Sex 2) Commitment 3) Spending Time 4) Communication.

148. Thou shall not gasp.

149. A man is only permitted to give another member of the man species a high-five during competitive activities or while viewing sporting events. Any other scenario must gain clearance from the society of Man Laws before being attempted.

150. Although man-on-man frisking is a man law violation, it is permitted for the best man to frisk all bachelor party attendees for cameras and camcorders.

151. If it itches, it will be scratched.

152. It is understood that thou cannot control one's dreams, however, a man should not characteristically be in another man's dream. If said occurrence does transpire, thou shall not communicate the incident with the male dream specimen or any other living human being for that matter. In fact, a man must be comfortable with taking said dream to his grave.

153. It is a rare occurrence that two buddies show up to an outing or event wearing the same or similar articles of clothing. However, it is forbidden for two men to plan to dress alike. Extreme consequences shall result in such a violation.

154.   It is common practice for buddies to vacation together at destination hot spots in an effort to further their conquest of the female species. However economical it may seem, it is highly frowned upon to share the same hotel room.

155.   While under the influence, it is common practice for a group of social hipsters to engage in interactive team games. However, the ratio of guys to girls has to favor the girls to play the following games: Spin The Bottle, Truth or Dare, and/or Twister™.

156.   If a woman asks a man if he has any cute friends, he must gently "mush" her face until said damsel is able to conjure up another question.

157.   Hey man, remember when you were younger and you had a favorite color? Remember? Remember? Of course you don't.

158.   Men don't complain. They pretty much just tend to roll with the

punches. So to avoid confusion, while texting or social networking, thou shall not use multiple question marks to add emphasis to any question or request. Ok???

159. If a lady has had a wardrobe malfunction; before the gentleman card can be played, every man in the vicinity must catch a glance before thou can say "hey your boob is loose". By vicinity, we're talking about a quarter mile radius.

160. In busy New York style pedestrian traffic, it is suggested to keep at least a 4 foot cushion when walking behind another able bodied man, just in case said man needs to stop to tie his shoe.

161. As a man, there shall never cometh a time where you find an opportunity to call another man "mean".

162. Upon the dreadful instance that you're asked to accompany a member of the lady gender on a

shopping binge, shopping bags belong in your hands, not on thine shoulders.

163. Laugh like a man. Men don't giggle.

164. A man's shirt and pants should never be of the same material, pattern or color.

165. No personal phone conversations of any length shall be permitted past 10pm with any buddy. If one buddy is in another time zone while the other is past 10pm in an alternate time zone, divide the sum of the difference by 3, then multiply by hanging up the phone.

166. In the frequent instance that a man must apologize to avoid excruciating circumstances, the childish shenanigan of crossing your fingers always makes it easier to utter a more realistic "I'm sorry".

167. Never shall a man wear the socks with the individual toes.

168. Never tell another man above the age of 14 that his singing voice is amazing.

169. As a man, the only time it's permissible to utter the sound "awww" is immediately and aggressively before an expletive. Awww &%#@!!!

170. It's not common practice to prepare another man's plate above the age of 10.

171. Being a professional or avid bowler makes you a man with a cool hobby. However, it doesn't make you an athlete.

172. While cheating is not condoned by the commission of Man Laws, it does happen. In the instance that a man breaks the code of silence and admits to infidelity, said man shall be permitted to pay every man in the Western Hemisphere a one dollar restitution fee.

173. When referring to a female companion whom thine shared the most platonic moments with,

you cannot and shall not refer to the dame as your "bestie" or "bff".

174. Umbrellas are not banned, but definitely not encouraged.

175. In the instance that there are two men, two seats and one armrest, one arm will rest. Driver takes priority.

176. Studies show that men cheerleaders suffer from a severe testosterone deficiency and cannot be biologically or practically be referred to as men.

177. While it can be very manly to have tattoos, it is in no way manly for a man to have a tattoo on thine lower back, foot or ankle.

178. A man purse is still a purse.

179. No man shall dance for recreation unless it's to improve his stake with a member of the opposite sex.

180.   If a lion shall catch a man off guard and bites said man, he is allowed to scream, once.

181.   Biker shorts are not underwear, but should always be worn "under" something. In most cases it can be shorts. Even if thou is the greatest cyclist in thou hemisphere you cannot wear biker shorts stand alone.

182.   If a man shall not sweat during a particular activity, said activity can not be deemed a sport. Please note that most men sweat during Beer Pong.

183.   The only time a man should catch thine legs crossed is when scaling an electrical wire attempting to escape prison.

184.   The man capacity of any revolving door is one.

185.   Once a man has relinquished possession of the TV remote control to a female specimen, he is subliminally telling her that, in less than five minutes, he will be exiting stage left.

186. A man is allowed to engage in a maximum of two 30+ minute phone conversations per female that he dates, as long as said damsel is doing 75% of the talking.

187. When picking players for sports teams, it is permissible for a man to skip over thine buddy in favor of better athletes, as long as you don't allow him be amongst the final two outcasts amongst on the sideline.

188. A man shall never join thine girlfriend in ragging on a buddy... unless said damsel is withholding sex, pending thine rebuttal.

189. Roadside assistance is necessary for a dead battery, but not for changing a flat tire, or running out of gas, unless the nearest gas station is more than 7 miles away.

190. While it may be less than fashionable these days, it is ok to buy clothing a size or two bigger, however, it will never be ok to

buy or wear clothing a size or
two smaller.

191. Every man cave must contain
enough food, beer, and cable to
last up to 12 hours at a time.

192. Thou should never possess the
ability to recognize your buddy
from behind.

193. Band-aids were never intended
for men. Anything not requiring
stitches should be left exposed,
to heal naturally.

194. Real men pray.

195. Men don't buy pajamas. If a man
shall receive them as a typical
holiday gift, it is permissible to
occasionally wear them to
appease the gifter. The act of a
man "changing clothes" to go to
bed is just not permissible on a
daily basis.

196. Chips and beer have one thing in
common. You can't have just
one.

197. When getting a haircut, a man
must keep his arms, inside the

armrests. For women reading
this book, know that only a man
shall comprehend this one.

198. A man shall never make a bet he
can't honor.

199. Once a man purchases a 12 pack
of beer, it is to be consumed in a
72 hour window. Otherwise, said
man should have purchased a 6
pack.

200. When a man happens to spot a
dame consuming a banana,
sucker, popsicle or hot dog, it is
customary to stop, enjoy a brief
daydream, emit a drizzle of
drool, make a chauvinistic
comment, and/or all of the
above.

201. Men and instructional booklets
go together like women and
monster trucks.

202. When walking, men's shoes shall
not be "heard".

203. A man shall never be deemed too
old to play war-based or sports
video games.

204.   A toilet bowl is a man's throne.
        Some of thine best meditation
        will occur during this final act of
        digestion. Never shall a man be
        interrupted while performing
        such divine excretion. Thus,
        should be complemented with a
        fully secure bathroom facility
        complete with a deadbolt locking
        door.

205.   Men over the age of 13 ½ shall
        not play the flute.

206.   A mentally healthy man shall
        never dress a dog in clothing,
        including but not limited to the
        following: cardigan sweaters,
        bonnets, footsies, scarves, tutus,
        hoodies, rain coats, etc.

207.   If a man takes an oath or makes
        a promise while under the
        influence, it is to be considered
        small talk and said man should
        not be held accountable to honor
        any such drunken promise.

208.   When a man is questioned by his
        buddy's wife, said man should
        express that he hath failed in
        communication attempts to

reach him since the last known communication with his wife.

209. Men don't dance alone at nightclubs. Needless to say, they also don't dance with each other.

210. Body paint originated in a small town named Green Bay and was accompanied by a funny looking hat made of cheese; and this was considered extremely manly. Unless accompanied by a helmet with Viking horns or any other funny looking headpiece, body paint is strictly prohibited.

211. One of the greatest jobs a man can have is being a photographer. Particularly in the area of swimsuit models.

212. If a man's vehicle cannot efficiently transport a 60 inch television, it is safe to say said man is driving a car built for a chick.

213. A woman nagging is the equivalent to a man cheating.

214. After working an eight hour shift, a married man is entitled

to his choice of immediate sex, an indulgent home cooked meal, or both. If denied any of the above, said man can opt for a three hour stint at the bar of his choice.

215.   Fruit is healthy, but fruity drinks are highly unhealthy to the male species.

216.   Anything more than two handshakes between males in one social setting is too many. That would represent "hi" and "goodbye". In instances of exciting news, three such displays of male affection is the absolute limit.

217.   A man doesn't typically remember another man's birthday until Facebook™ posts a notification about it.

218.   Men are not allowed to wish happy birthday to another man until after 1pm the day of said man's birthday. Phone calls right when the clock strikes 12 midnight are strictly prohibited.

219. Men shall enjoy particular television shows, but no man shall express that he has a "favorite" show.

220. It should take a man no longer than 15 minutes to get ready for anything. This includes taking a shower, shaving, and getting dressed. This excludes toilet time. A man's toilet time shall have no limit.

221. A man shall not sport gloves as a fashion accessory. Excluding Michael Jackson.

222. Michael Jordan™ is the greatest basketball player that ever lived.

223. Men's toes don't belong in public.

224. If a man shall accidentally spill another man's beer, he is permitted to buy him another. If the spillage was done purposely, thou hath just declared war.

225. The title "stay at home dad" is only used in fictional novels and Lifetime™ movies.

226. The word "scream" shall never be preceded by the preposition "he" nor "I" when the gender of the person speaking in first person is a male specimen.

227. A man shall not "flick" anything under the sun. Men throw or heave things. When playing catch with a member of the male species that is under the age of 11, it is ok to "toss". When the male species obtains the ability to rise above the sun, this rule shall be amended.

228. There are certain words or phrases that by definition, should exclude any male gender reference. Including but not limited to: "freaking out", "prissy", "prance", "fabulous", "nag", "irritable", "bourgeois", "shopaholic", "dainty", "giggle", "shapely", "bootylicious" and "frolic".

229. There are certain men that are permitted to have long hair, such as bikers, Rastafarians and Fabio. But no man with such a

lengthy grade of hair shall ever make a "hair appointment".

230.   There is not one man walking on Earth who can give a review of a romance novel. Not even a professional book critic.

231.   No man shall be permitted to watch any television show with the word "girls" included in the title.

232.   Hunting is not a coed sport or activity.

233.   As a man, it is ok to have never shot a gun before. However, it's not very customary to be carefree about admitting it.

234.   Men over the age of 10 don't swing. On a date at a park, a man is fully permitted to push a female companion on the swings, but said man is not permitted to join her in swinging.

235.   For some reason, a man's exposed butt crack can be deemed manly, but only if said man is tightening pipes, and is

unaware of such bottom cleavage.

236. A man on roller skates must be accompanied by a female skater who is a noticeably better skater. It is even encouraged to take a few tumbles along your path to prove this fact.

237. The only time that two or more men should be seen ice skating together is during a hockey game or practice. Never during a "rehearsal".

238. A man shall never refer to his pectoral muscles as "breasts".

239. Although the syllable "man" is in the word manicure, it doesn't give any man permission to... (Do you kind of see where we're going with this?)

240. Trash is a very manly word. Men often engage in "trash" talk during sport. It's a man's duty to take out the "trash". And finally, certain men often seek out "trashy" girls.

241.   Men don't purchase outfits or articles of clothing for specific events. Men rarely premeditate any fashionable purchase.

242.   It's not too often that you shall find two men in a bedroom together. But you shall never find an able bodied man relaxing, laying or sitting atop another man's bed. Even if said man lives in a dorm room or studio apartment.

243.   Men are not allowed to go to an ice cream parlor unless accompanied by one or more female counterparts.

244.   Men shall not plan to go to a karaoke night at a bar. If said men plan to go to a bar and it happens to be karaoke night, it is totally permissible.

245.   When buying flowers for a lady friend, a man is not permitted to sniff or smell the petals until after said damsel requests that he smells how nice they are.

246.   While it isn't the manliest
        activity, it is permissible for a
        man to join his church's choir.
        But what isn't permissible is
        requesting to be in the alto
        section to showcase your range.

247.   It is customary for men to hi-five
        each other during extremely
        competitive activities. It is cool
        for a man to hi-five a woman for
        any reason. A hetero man giving
        a hi-five to an openly gay man
        for any non-sports related
        activity.... is simply not ideal.

248.   Men shall not whistle songs
        originally performed by female
        recording artists.

249.   Bananas can be a healthy part of
        a man's balanced diet. However
        a man shall not just peel and
        consume. Proper procedure is to
        peel, slice multiple times, then
        eat. Please adhere to a five slice
        minimum.

250.   There is nothing wrong with a
        man wanting to be clean, but any
        man that takes more than two
        showers on any given day may

be eligible to lose his man
privileges.

251.   Men don't compare body parts
amongst each other.

252.   If a man is dumped by his
girlfriend, a six month waiting
period must go into effect before
any of his buddies are allowed to
make a pass. If said man is the
one who dumps his girlfriend,
then a seven day waiting period
goes into effect. This law does
not apply to wives or long-term
girlfriends of three years or
more.

253.   Thou hath not seen the film
Brokeback Mountain™. Even if
you think you may have, thou
hath not.

254.   There aren't too many instances
when a man shall have to cross
thine legs. Maybe right before a
spin move on a dance floor. But
then again, there aren't too
many instances when a man
shall have to do a spin move on a
dance floor.

255. Men don't usually complain about being cold. They just grin and bear it.

256. Men are generally very competitive by nature; especially in the area of sports, but not so much in the area of fashion. If another man asks you where you got a particularly cool tie from, just tell him.

257. It is not in a man's nature to eavesdrop. Therefore it is not permissible unless said man happens to overhear someone trolling his favorite sports team; then he gets a pass.

258. When sitting in a chair, it is frowned upon for any man's posture to resemble that of an acute geometric angle. However, obtuse angles are widely accepted in man land everywhere. And you thought you would never get to use geometry in real life.

259. For young men under the age of 10, it doesn't hurt until you see blood.

260. For men over the age of 10, it doesn't hurt until a bone has been completely broken, or a body part has been completely severed. Seeing blood is not the indicator to begin to feel pain.

261. When asked to play a pickup game of flag football, one must at least portray as if he is agitated about it not being tackle rules.

262. A short tie accompanied by an unbuttoned jacket is never a great idea.

263. Picture this: Your phone rings, but it's on the other side of the room. It's your pal from work. How do you know this without going to answer it? Please, no ringtones shall be reserved for another male who is not a member of your immediate family.

264. "Pretty please" is never authorized to emit from a grown man's mouth. Please never say, write, text, or sign language this.

265. A man will never inherit an
honest answer regarding the
number of his spouse's previous
intimate partners. And more
than likely, if her answer is
above a six (plus the two to four
she feels like shouldn't have
counted,) thine ego probably
can't handle it.

266. Men are only allowed to shave
once per day.

267. When at an outdoor event, such
as a large picnic, it is more
common to see an overweight
beer-bellied guy barbecuing
shirtless than it is to see an in
shape buffed guy just standing
around with his shirt off.

268. Men are not allowed to get road
rage from seeing another man
driving too fast.

269. When a man purchaseth a new
home, said man is not allowed to
purchase a dining room set
before purchasing a lawn mower
and/or barbeque grill.

270. Men either swim, or don't swim. Men don't doggy paddle.

271. A man shall never enter on a bet in which he can't immediately deliver on the amount wagered if deemed the loser.

272. There shall never come an instance where a man shall find the desire to walk with a "skip."

273. The only recorded incidents where men have been allowed to cross their legs is while sitting in a tatami room at a Japanese restaurant.

274. A man shall not admit to anything being "spooky".

275. The only object a man can find pretty is a woman. Not that women are objects, but in this context it works, for men.

276. As long as men allow women to think they are the smarter gender, life will be easier.

277. All men are allowed one attempt at seeing how fast their car can really go. Male law enforcement

is aware of this law. If pulled over by a female cop, just admit guilt and refer to Law 281.

278.   Men under 50 must jog, run, ride a bike, or play a sport for exercise. Going for "a walk" is not permitted in the exercise category. It is, however, permitted in the "I just had an argument with my wife and need to step away before I do or say something I really regret" category.

279.   When met at a red light by a female motorist, it is a man's duty to leave her in the dust. And by "leave her in the dust" we mean, have crossed the intersection before said female driver even pulls off.

280.   Here's a list of things a man must have done before the age of 18: Climbed a tree, played tackle football, bench pressed 30 pounds over his own weight, and gone a couple days without showering.

281. Here's a list of things a man must have done before the age of 30: Built something cool worth showing his buddies, driven at least 90 miles per hour, have hit a homerun, and have read the book "365 Man Laws to Live By."

282. Here's a list of things a man must have done before the age of 50: Have bought a home, have built a brand new deck for that home, have instilled fear in his daughter's boyfriend, and cooked on a barbeque grill for at least 10 or more people.

283. A man is not allowed to end a fishing trip without catching at least one sizeable fish.

284. Married or not, a man is not allowed to watch two romantic comedies in a row.

285. It takes seven years from the breakup of the boy band for any member to be accepted back into the man kingdom.

286. Men don't sub-tweet.

287.   Even if a man were born with a higher pitched voice than normal, in order to keep his man status, he is only allowed to sing in the tenor or baritone section of the local church choir. Fake it till you make it.

288.   Men are not allowed to pass other men in theater rows or church pews. If a man shall insist on exiting the row, each man that shall be passed must rise and exit the row to avoid said awkward pass.

289.   Since men are not allowed to take baths, a bubble bath is certainly out of the question.

290.   Sometimes a popsicle can be a nice cool treat during the summer. If a man is to consume a popsicle, it must be bitten and chewed, never sucked or licked.

291.   Men with painting skills are not allowed to paint portraits of other men.

292.   Two men are not allowed to enjoy the same beverage. If ever

a man shall here the following request from another man "Aye man, let me get a sip of that", said sipper shall respond by turning thine back and taking 30 paces south.

293. If in a bind where a man can't get out of purchasing women's sanitary napkins for his wife, one must make his best effort in concealing said box of women sponges until check out. If additional purchases are necessary to assist in concealing in shopping cart, then so be it.

294. Unless an immediate family member, or a close friend is on his deathbed, never is a man allowed to look into another man's eyes and utter, "I Love You Man".

295. Never shall a man compliment another man on his jeans.

296. Men don't borrow clothes from other men.

297. Never dedicate a book entitled "365 Man Laws to Live By" to your wife.

298. Men don't get pedicures.

299. No matter how stressed a man has become, never is he allowed to receive a shoulder rub from another able bodied man.

300. The only time a man is allowed to put dye in thine hair is to conceal embarrassing grey hairs.

301. The only man on earth that a man can think is handsome is himself.

302. Making eye contact with another man while singing any song is strictly forbidden.

303. A man must exercise a 24 hour waiting period before kissing a girl that he has physically seen kissing another man. Anything under 24 hours will be considered a man on man kiss.

304. At the gym, a man is not allowed to get on a bike machine within

5 minutes of another sweat-filled man getting off.

305.   A man shall not take mirror pictures with thine cell phone.

306.   Men either swear or they don't. A man shall not abbreviate or insinuate a swear word.

307.   At a restaurant, a man shall eat what he orders. Men should never have to say the words "doggie bag" out loud in a public place.

308.   As a man, thou shall never feel the need to quote Oprah.

309.   Men shall not go to concerts headlined by female acts unless begged, threatened or blackmailed by their lady friend.

310.   If over the age of 17, a man cannot be a victim of bullying. It's called getting an old fashioned butt kicking.

311.   Before calling a professional repairman, a man shall make at least two valiant attempts at do-it-yourself repairs.

312.   Men don't buy candles or an air freshener.

313.   If a man finds a bug or insect inside the four walls of his home, it is his lawful duty to seek and destroy said tiny intruder.

314.   Men cannot express that any object is "beautiful" other than a woman who is above a seven on a scale from one to 10.

315.   If a man all of a sudden decides to quit thines 9 to 5 to pursue a career as a rap superstar, and decides it would be good publicity to do a "diss record", thou must include the disrespected victim's name into the recording.

316.   A man shall not scream, gasp, jump or holler while watching a scary movie. Actually, there's no such thing as a scary movie. It's just a movie.

317.   A man shall not hang thine feet outside the window of moving car.

318. Unless sitting with a doctor in a doctor's office, a man shall never find the need to refer to his chest.

319. While wearing a buttoned shirt, a man must not allow more than three buttons to be unbuttoned from the top down.

320. Men use lotion but they don't "moisturize".

321. Even though it's acceptable to save on high gas prices, thou shall at least cringe at the suggestion of having to carpool.

322. If it looks like a purse, it's still a purse. Men don't need purses.

323. A man's nails may never extend past thine finger tips. There is nothing worse than exchanging a "homie handshake" with a male specimen and his elongated nails.

324. Two or more males are not permitted to go horseback riding together.

325. A man shall never express
      outward excitement upon his
      buddy arriving at a place or
      event.

326. A man's Man cave must be
      constructed so that thine female
      counterparts need an eye scan,
      thumb print and access code to
      gain entry.

327. Thou shall not display evidence
      of continual and/or consecutive
      inside jokes with thine male
      counterparts. Especially when
      there are other folks above the
      age of 12 present.

328. Modern, thinner cans make the
      feat of crushing of empty beer
      cans or your forehead less
      impressive than with cans of
      years past.

329. If a man liveth at home with
      thine mother, it's never an okay
      feat to sleep naked.

330. When at the gym, a man is not
      allowed to ask another man for a
      spot unless said weight is more

than 10% more than the lifters's overall body weight.

331. Regardless of body fat percentage, a man shall never be embarrassed to disrobe in the presence of his lady friend. Confidence shall always prevail.

332. A man must never refer to his lady as a his "significant other".

333. Although not encouraged, it is acceptable for a man to gain employment as a nurse, however, it is not acceptable for a man to be the nurse while engaging in role play with thine lady.

334. A man must never tend to the grooming of thine facial hair longer than it takes to brush thine teeth.

335. Men use their pinky finger for absolutely nothing.

336. Men are not allowed to set the mood with music before they attempt to clean, unless the musical piece is "Eye of the Tiger™" and they mix a little

shadow boxing in with thine vacuuming.

337. Two men sitting at one table must sit 180 degrees from each other. For those of you who failed geometry, that's 12 o'clock and 6 o'clock.

338. If there are 3 urinals, and none are occupied, it is an extreme violation for a man to choose thine middle one.

339. Men are never allowed to fan themselves with thine hands, or any fan-like object for that matter.

340. Two or more buddies shall never plan to wear the same cologne.

341. Men shall use as much slang as possible when communicating with one another. For example, when one wishes to say "hey may I ride with you to the party?", the appropriate dialect should be "sup bro... cool if I roll witcha to the spot?"

342. A man shall never mentally or physically like another man's selfie on social media.

343. A man shall not post more than one selfie per month. A selfie constitutes as a self-portrait photograph, typically taken with a hand-held digital camera or camera phone.

344. It is understood that a Febreezed sheet is just as good as a sheet fresh from the laundry.

345. When a man is eating a banana in public, he must break said banana into multiple bite-sized pieces for convenient consumption.

346. Body wash for men is still body wash. This product is usually intended for women with unusually hairy legs.

347. When a man is asked to watch a chick-flick with his female counterpart, he must make said female agree to watch one action film as repayment.

348. Whether right or wrong, when a group of guys are debating with a group of women, no male involved can be persuaded, coerced or convinced to jump ship and see the point the females are trying to make.

349. As a man, it is unacceptable to cool off your coffee or other hot beverage by blowing it in public. Thou shall just have to play the waiting game until able to comfortably consume.

350. Casual phone conversations between two or more men are perfectly acceptable under ten minutes. Video calls, chats or messaging is completely unnecessary and will be deemed a violation of Man Law.

351. For some reason, conversations between leafless men in a locker room are only acceptable when the bare-bottomed specimens are beyond the age of 65.

352.   Here's the situation. There's two men, one beverage, and both are extremely parched. Unless in a life threatening situation, such as stranded on a deserted island, one will suffer. Sharing is not an option.

353.   Unless you're a black comedian, wearing an all leather outfit is forbidden.

354.   The views and opinions expressed inside the men's locker room, shall without a doubt, stay there.

355.   Thou shall never assist another able-bodied male in putting on thine seatbelt.

356.   Upon the instance of you spotting your buddy's girl cheating on him, you take a picture and immediately send to your buddy. Upon the instance of you spotting your buddy cheating on this girl, you make sure that your phone is nowhere to be found.

357. Men don't wave at each other. Waving constitutes wiggling fingers and men do not, and will not do that.

358. Upon the unfortunate circumstance that a man is fired, Man Law states that said man must give himself a ten day grace period of freedom and the opportunity of finding a new job before he can inform his wife. If said man is not married and dating a female counterpart, he is not obligated to saying anything until the cows come home.

359. Regardless of a complete blowout, during the Superbowl™ and other key televised sporting events, a man is forbidden from texting or calling any female specimen for non emergencies. This is to keep continuity in banning female distractions during televised games.

360. If your buddy is engaged in a conversation with an unknown attractive female specimen, a

man must give said buddy two interrupted minutes to seal the deal. If the female is a known associate, then 30 seconds shall be granted. If the female is unattractive, then an immediate distraction is encouraged.

361. When a man is shoveling show, he should always keep the handle above waist level or he may regret when said shovel hits a fault in the pavement and comes to a sudden stop.

362. If two men are hungry at the same time and that time happens to be between the hours of 10:00 am and 11:00 am, they have the green light to go grab a bite to eat, but, with that said, men don't do "brunch".

363. Men may use coupons to save money, but a man shall never engage in "couponing".

364. Men may do yoga; but are forbidden from wearing "yoga pants".